Skulduggery Pleasant

APOCALYPSE KINGS

Not suitable for younger readers

WORLD BOOK DAY

DEREK LANDY

APOCALYPSE KINGS

HarperCollins *Children's Books*

First published in Great Britain by
HarperCollins *Children's Books* in 2021
HarperCollins *Children's Books* is a division of HarperCollins*Publishers* Ltd,
1 London Bridge Street
London SE1 9GF

www.harpercollins.co.uk

HarperCollins*Publishers*
1st Floor, Watermarque Building, Ringsend Road
Dublin 4, Ireland

1

Typeset in Baskerville MT 11/13.5 pt by
Palimpsest Book Production Ltd, Falkirk, Stirlingshire

Printed and bound in England by CPI Group (UK) Ltd, Croydon CR0 4YY
A CIP catalogue record for this title is available from the British Library.

There are no animals featured in this book, and yet this book is dedicated to a whole lot of them.

This is to Groomer and Sansa and Bowie and Lorelai and Rory and Salem and Tilly, for all the love and all the laughs.

And this book is also dedicated to the pets that have been lost over the years – so this is to Ziggy, to Sylvester, to Mammy Cat, to Pooper, to Sherlock, to Mabel and to Ali – the inspiration for Xena and the greatest dog who ever lived.

To all the good girls and all the good boys. If you have a pet, you are their whole world, so love them accordingly. If you don't have a pet but you have a younger sibling, pretend they're a kitten and love them too. Also, dress them up in stupid outfits and laugh at them.

For isn't that what Christmas is REALLY all about?

1

Adedayo was fourteen when he discovered that he was magic.

Up until then, he'd lived what he reckoned to be a normal life. He was on the school football team, which he enjoyed. He was on the school debating team, which he didn't. He had his family, he had his friends, he liked dogs but was wary of cats, he didn't like spiders, he hated rats and he ran away from wasps. All pretty normal. All pretty standard.

The magic thing happened over the course of a few weeks, when things started to come to him. Not answers, or knowledge, or insight, or anything like that – but actual *things*. Lamps, and bottles of water and big, heavy books. They'd fly at him as soon as he looked at them and he'd have to duck or jump back or run screaming from the room.

At first, Adedayo thought he was being haunted. Then he thought that he must have annoyed an invisible man at some point. One afternoon, after a teapot had collided with his face, he covered the kitchen floor in flour and waited for a footprint to appear. His mother appeared first, of course, and yelled at him, told him to clean it up. Adedayo was more scared of his mum than he was of an invisible man, so he did what he was told and wondered why he was being singled out for torment by this invisible gentleman when his two younger sisters were way more annoying than he ever managed to be.

Then his grandmother came to stay. She was a small Nigerian woman who didn't speak much English, but her health wasn't the best and she couldn't stay on her own any more. Adedayo's sisters were told they had to share a room and their grandmother – their beloved *ìyá agba* – moved in. It took some time to adjust to a new person in the house, but she was lovely, so nobody minded, and a few weeks later she knocked on Adedayo's door.

Adedayo didn't speak much Yoruba, his grandmother's language. His parents were both English speakers and, once they'd moved to Ireland to start a family, that's how they'd raised him and his sisters. They'd tried to teach him a few words over the years, but he didn't have much interest in learning, so, when his grandmother sat beside him on the bed, he prepared himself for a few long, long minutes of hesitations and the slow searching for words in English that always accompanied the rather pointless stories of her childhood. But she was his *ìyá agba*, and he loved her, so Adedayo smiled and pretended with all his heart to be interested in whatever she had to say.

She surprised him, then, by telling him something so brain-punchingly interesting that it changed his life forever.

She told him, in that hesitant way of hers, that magic was real, and that she was magic, and so was he.

At first, he thought she was just telling him a story to entertain him, but when she clicked her fingers and conjured a fireball into her hand it all started to make sense. The odd occurrences, the weird coincidences, the objects that moved on their own – that was magic. His grandmother explained that there were rules for people like them; there were styles of magic he could specialise in, other magical people – sorcerers, or mages – he could meet. She told him about the Sanctuaries around the world, and the wars that had been fought between the sorcerers who wanted to enslave ordinary people and the sorcerers who wanted to protect them.

He had such a life ahead of him, she said. Such wonders to uncover.

She taught him some things – how to move objects by manipulating the air around them; how to make strands of energy dance in the palms of his hands; how to click his fingers and generate sparks. She told him about the three names that sorcerers have – the name they're given, the name they take, and their true name, the source of all their power.

But she was an old, old woman, and, a few weeks after his fifteenth birthday, her health deteriorated so much she had to be taken to hospital. Her energy dipped so that she lost all of her English and could only speak the language of her childhood. When Adedayo went in to sit with her, she woke, took his hand and said weakly, "*Má şi àpótí.*" Then she smiled, and closed her eyes.

Má şi àpótí, he repeated in his head. *Má şi àpótí.* He made a note to ask his folks what that meant, but it slipped his mind, and his grandmother passed away later that night, and Adedayo was left with a lifetime of questions, a heart full of grief and a polished wooden box.

His grandmother had insisted that it had to go to him, apparently. That only he would know what to do with it.

The box was the size of a biscuit tin. It had carvings across the lid and along the sides – carvings that looked like letters, that looked like words, but weren't. There was no lock, no latch, no way to open it. There was nothing inside, though. Or there didn't seem to be when Adedayo's mum shook it. His dad tried prising the lid off with a screwdriver. Didn't work.

The wooden box had been sitting on Adedayo's desk, under a pile of pristine textbooks and dog-eared graphic novels, for weeks when Adedayo woke in the middle of the night, suddenly *knowing* how to open it.

He got out of bed, crossed the dark room and cleared the junk off the lid. He tapped the carvings on the box's left and right sides, then pressed, then tapped again and moved his fingers in a swirling motion.

A dim blue light shone from between the carvings, travelling across the box in strange, swirling patterns. There were sounds from inside, like wooden cogs turning.

And then there was a click.

2

Suddenly apprehensive, and not a little nervous, Adedayo ever so slowly lifted the lid. Inside was dark. Inside was empty.

But something in that emptiness reached out and Adedayo went rigid, his fingers splayed, his legs locked straight, his head back and the muscles in his neck standing out. He felt a consciousness, more than one, poking through his mind, picking out his language, sorting through what he knew of the world, and then his knees wobbled and he went floppy and staggered back a few steps before collapsing.

A hand emerged from the box.

The hand became a forearm and then there was an elbow, and the elbow pressed down on the table for leverage and a shoulder appeared and then a head, a head with a black veil and horns poking out, a head far too big to be squeezing through a box the size of a biscuit tin.

This thing, this being, was called the Sathariel. Adedayo

didn't know how he knew that – he just did. It was like there was a swimming pool full of weird knowledge and he'd just cannonballed into it. He watched the Sathariel climb out of the box and stand by the table, his black robes long and ragged, his breathing heavy, his horns sharp.

He had mottled green hands tipped with black nails, and from his robes he drew a gnarled staff as tall as he was. The smell he brought with him was pungent and made Adedayo think of people screaming.

Something else came out of the box: a tentacle, wet and dripping. It probed the air, then found the table, and a second one came out to join it, then another. Then there were a dozen tentacles, some as thin as a cat's tongue, some as thick as an elephant's trunk, and once they'd gained purchase they lifted the Cythraul straight up out of the box.

The Cythraul, the Many-Tentacled One, hid most of his body beneath a robe of soiled crimson, but Adedayo caught a flash of pale, squirming flesh that made his stomach roil. The Cythraul had a wide, gaping mouth lined with small, sharp teeth, like a lamprey eel, and a single black, blinking eye. He looked down at Adedayo and then, thankfully, away.

There was another creature in the box. The last of the Apocalypse Kings unfurled himself from his confinement and stepped into the bedroom. Tall and thin, black-haired and pale, long-faced and red-eyed, the

Deathless wore a robe of rags and filth that fitted him like kingly vestments.

He looked round Adedayo's bedroom and breathed in, then smiled.

"Smells like feet," he said, and all three of them vanished.

3

For reasons both completely outrageous and totally under-standable, Adedayo found it hard to concentrate in school the next day.

He had said nothing to his parents or his sisters about the creatures that had emerged from the box. He had said nothing to them about anything, in fact. His *ìyá agbà* had told him that his sisters might develop magical abil-ities as they got older and, if they did, it would be his job to guide them. But, until that happened, it was safer to keep the truth from ordinary people. Safer for them, and safer for Adedayo.

He'd walked to school, met up with his friends, wearing a smile and laughing when the others laughed, but not paying one bit of attention to what anyone was saying. As he sat in class, he ignored the teachers and stared at the pages of his books and worried – for there was a lot to worry about.

The first lesson of the day was given over to debating practice, in which Adedayo performed even worse than usual. He'd joined the team because he needed at least *one* extracurricular activity for when he eventually applied to university, but he wasn't very good at debating. He found it difficult to come up with a coherent argument at the best of times, and this was certainly not the best of times.

The hours passed in a confusing, hazy blur, and suddenly Adedayo was in maths, the last lesson of the day, his eyes on a long line of equations the class had to solve. There was a knock on the door.

"Hello," a girl said, coming in without waiting for an invitation.

She was around Adedayo's age, fifteen or so. Taller than him, with long dark hair. She was wearing the school uniform, but he didn't recognise her.

"Yes?" said Mr Hopkins, frowning with irritation. He didn't like his lessons being interrupted.

"Hi there," said the girl. She had a nice confident smile. "I was wondering if I could speak to Adedayo Akinde."

Everyone looked at Adedayo, except for Mr Hopkins, whose frown deepened. "Who?"

"*Adedayo Akinde*," the girl repeated.

"No, no, who wants to speak to him? The principal? Another teacher?"

"Oh," the girl said, and laughed. "No, only me."

Mr Hopkins blinked at her. "Are you a student here?"

"Yes, exactly. I'm new, though. I just need Adedayo for a moment. Maybe two moments. Three at the very most."

"I don't know how they did things in your last school, young lady, but here we don't have pupils calling on other pupils in the middle of classes."

She didn't respond right away. She just looked at him as if she couldn't understand why he wasn't simply doing what she wanted. "I'm sorry," she said, "I think we got off on the wrong foot. I need to speak to Adedayo. Thank you." She turned to the class. "Adedayo, are you here?"

Once more, everyone looked at Adedayo, but he put up his hand anyway, and the girl smiled.

"A word?" she said, indicating the doorway.

Adedayo stood, but Mr Hopkins was quicker. "Adedayo, you are not to leave this room. Young lady, unless I get a full explanation—"

"What is this class?" the girl asked. "Maths? I'm a maths prodigy. I'm so far beyond genius that they don't even have a word for what I am. People like me have a club, and we think Adedayo might belong in it."

Mr Hopkins looked insultingly sceptical. "You think Adedayo is a maths prodigy? Adedayo, what do you think of this idea?"

"Um," said Adedayo.

"That's what I thought."

"The problem with prodigies such as ourselves," said the girl, "is that mainstream schools fail to challenge us, and, in doing so, fail to recognise our vast, vast intellects."

Mr Hopkins folded his arms. "And do you have anything to back up these claims of yours?"

The girl walked over to the whiteboard, picked up a red marker and started writing a sequence of bracketed numbers. She wore a thick black ring on one of the fingers of her right hand. "This equation, for super-geniuses, is as easy as falling into a ditch, and, if you've ever fallen into a ditch, you'll know how easy that is. If you, or anyone in this class, come even close to solving it by the time I've finished talking to Adedayo, that'll be all the proof you'll need." She popped the lid back on the marker and tossed it to Mr Hopkins. "Adedayo, out here, please."

Adedayo didn't know what to do, so he hurried into the corridor.

"I'm a maths genius?" he asked once the girl had shut the door behind them.

"What?" she said, glancing at her watch. "Oh, God, no. I mean, maybe you are. Are you? I haven't a clue. I hate maths. Always have. Too many numbers."

"Then what was that equation you wrote on the board?"

"Complete gibberish," she said. "In fact, your teacher will figure that out in a few seconds, so do you mind if we walk as we talk? Thanks awfully."

She began to stride away, and Adedayo, unable to think of what else to do, followed her.

4

As they neared the end of the corridor, the new girl turned to him and smiled. "Adedayo, my name is Valkyrie Cain. I heard you had some interesting visitors last night."

He stopped. "How did you know about that?"

Valkyrie took his arm, started him moving again. "I'll explain everything later, I swear. Or maybe I won't. It kinda depends on the threat level we're facing, to be honest. But I'll tell you what we know, OK? It won't take long, because we don't know a huge amount. Three creatures appeared in your house last night and then promptly left."

She paused. "And that's it. That's as much as we know. Well, apart from the fact that these creatures – they're pretty bad news. But I probably don't have to tell you that. Do I? I probably don't."

"Who are you?"

"Like I said, my name's Valkyrie Cain. I'm the good guy."

They heard the door open behind them.

"We can run, if you like," she said, smiling, and broke

into a jog. Adedayo jogged alongside her round the next corner.

"Did they say anything, the creatures?" she asked. "Did they mention who they were, what they wanted, anything like that?"

"All they said was that my bedroom smelled of feet."

"Huh," Valkyrie said. "That's a little mean, isn't it? Even if your bedroom *does* smell of feet, they didn't have to say it. Didn't have to point it out. You know the problem with supernatural creatures? They're rude. Yes, a lot of them also want to kill humans and/or destroy the world, but I'd say their main problem is the rudeness."

"Where are we going?" Adedayo asked as they jogged past the balcony overlooking the sports hall.

"That way," said Valkyrie, nodding to the exit at the bottom of the stairs.

He slowed. "What? I can't leave school."

"Of course you can. You do it every day."

"But classes haven't ended. I'll get in trouble."

Valkyrie put a hand on his shoulder and led him down the stairs. "I used to worry about things like that," she said. "I used to worry about teachers and homework and detentions, and what other people thought of me, and what my friends said, and what to wear, and what music to listen to, and none of this is true. I didn't worry about any of that because I'm way too cool and always have been, but at least I've managed to distract you long enough for us to get outside."

She pushed open the doors and they emerged into the fresh air. Adedayo looked around, expecting a horde of teachers to come sprinting up. Instead, an empty crisp packet skipped lightly over the ground.

"Come along," said Valkyrie, and strode across the courtyard. He didn't know why, exactly, but he followed her. They passed the Old House, a tall, imposing building that used to be the main school a hundred years ago, but was now for staff only. They walked right by the window of the principal's office. No one saw them.

There was a big black car parked in the staff car park – an old-fashioned car that gleamed in the sunlight. No one else was around.

"You're a sorcerer, aren't you?" Adedayo asked.

Valkyrie looked at him, surprised. "You know about us?"

"My *ìyá agba* – I mean, my gran – told me. She said I'm one of you."

"Oh, thank God," Valkyrie said, laughing. "I hate having to explain to mortals that magic and monsters exist and yes, there are bad guys, but *we're* the good guys and please, please stop screaming. I hate when they scream, y'know? It's just so unnecessary."

"Totally," said Adedayo.

A man got out of the car – a tall man in a dark blue suit, with a crisp white shirt and a dark blue tie. His hands were gloved and he wore a hat, like a detective in an old black-and-white movie.

"Adedayo," said Valkyrie, "this is my partner, Skulduggery Pleasant."

Adedayo was about to remark on such an unusual name when Skulduggery Pleasant tapped his shirt, just over the collarbones, and his face melted, actually *melted*, flowing off his bare bones and disappearing beneath his collar, so that what Adedayo saw looking at him now was just a skull wearing a hat.

"Hello, Adedayo," the skeleton said, "very pleased to meet you."

And Adedayo screamed.

5

Skulduggery and Valkyrie waited for Adedayo to finish screaming. It took a few seconds.

"Excellent," Skulduggery said, opening the door and moving his seat forward. "In you get. We need to talk, and privacy is required."

Adedayo should probably have run away. Instead, he climbed in.

Skulduggery got back behind the wheel and Valkyrie slid into the passenger seat. The car started with a gentle purr, and they left the school grounds and turned on to the road.

"Um," said Adedayo, "are you kidnapping me?"

"No," Skulduggery said immediately.

"No," said Valkyrie.

"Absolutely not," Skulduggery said.

"Are we, though?" Valkyrie asked.

Skulduggery shook his head. "If he agrees to come with us of his own free will, then it's not kidnapping, it's a day out."

Valkyrie looked back at Adedayo and shrugged. "There you go."

"Cool," Adedayo said, trying to smile. "I just wanted to check. Could I ask what's going on? And also how are you a skeleton?"

"The story of how I became a skeleton is a long one," Skulduggery said. "Thankfully, it is also a really interesting one because it's about me. The year was 1690, and the war with Mevolent had reached—"

"We're just going to skip this," Valkyrie interrupted, "because, like we said, we don't have an awful lot of time. Skulduggery, Adedayo already knows about magic. He's one of us."

"Oh, good," said Skulduggery, turning right. "That cuts down on the tedious explanations and the screaming."

"I was just saying that."

"I don't know an awful lot, though," Adedayo pointed out. "*Iyá Agba*, my grandmother, she was magic and she taught me a few things in secret. The rest of my family don't know. Things like . . ." He clicked his fingers a few times, but nothing happened, and he frowned. "Usually sparks fly out."

"It can be difficult to make magic work when you're nervous or scared," Valkyrie said. "Or when people are trying to kill you."

Adedayo blinked. "Will people be trying to kill me?"

Valkyrie and Skulduggery glanced at each other.

"No," Valkyrie said unconvincingly.

"Adedayo," Skulduggery said, "we know a few psychics and they had some rather disturbing dreams last night. The details are rather vague, but they all saw three beings at your address, they saw you, and they saw these beings abruptly depart. Then they saw these three beings destroy everything and kill everyone on the planet. Pretty standard apocalyptic stuff, to be fair – but it's our job to make sure that doesn't happen. So that's why we're here. We visited your home first, of course. Don't worry, no one was there, but we did find a wooden box in your bedroom. This is where the creatures emerged from, I assume?"

Adedayo nodded. "My grandmother left the box to me."

"It will, with your permission, be examined by experts at a later date, but from what we've seen the box appears to be an ancient but incredibly sophisticated prison. It's quite astounding, really."

"You get excited about the weirdest things," Valkyrie muttered, before turning back to Adedayo. "What can you tell us about the creatures that climbed out of it?"

"Everything," said Adedayo.

Valkyrie frowned. "Everything?"

"I . . . I don't know exactly how to describe it, but I think they kinda looked into my head? To learn about the world and the language and stuff? But, when they looked in, I don't know, it's like they left the door open to their minds. So I went in. Only it was more like I was jumping into a swimming pool full of knowledge. It was amazing."

"Oh, Adedayo," said Skulduggery, taking another right, "you just might be my favourite person I've met since you got in the car. So who are they?"

"Gods," said Adedayo. "All these gods, countless gods, lived, like, billions of years ago. Then the people came and started worshipping them and sacrificing each other, and things were good – if you were a god. The worshipping was nice, but all those sacrificed souls were . . . nourishment, I suppose. They made the gods stronger. So then one race of gods would attack another, and wars broke out, and . . . Anyway, there was this one race, called the Faceless Ones—"

"We're acquainted," Valkyrie said.

"Oh," said Adedayo, "cool. So they hunted down and, like, eradicated all the other gods. Three races – the Cythraul, the Sathariel and the Deathless – were on the verge of being wiped out and they wanted to make sure that the Faceless Ones starved to death once they were gone. Just to, like, teach them a lesson or something. So each race sent one of their last survivors to kill all worshippers. The humans, basically. To cut off the source of souls, you know? But the Faceless Ones managed to trap them in a magical box, the box my grandmother had. They put it aside and forgot about it for all that time and . . . and then last night I opened it and let the Apocalypse Kings out. That's, I think, roughly what their, like, collective name is." He sagged. "I'm such an idiot."

"Hey," said Skulduggery. "Hey."

Adedayo looked up. "Yes?"

"Hey," Skulduggery said again.

Valkyrie glared at the skeleton, then smiled at Adedayo. "You're not an idiot. There's no way you could have known what was in that box or what would happen once you opened it. I mean, it's a box. Boxes are meant to be opened."

"I know another lady who said that," Skulduggery muttered, turning right again. "Her name was Pandora and things did not go well for her."

"Oh, really?" Valkyrie said. "You knew Pandora, did you?"

"Yes," he responded. "Pandora Willoughby-Smythe, a very nice English lady who owned a rather nasty Pomeranian that got itself locked in a trunk one sunny afternoon. When she finally let it out, it had peed all over her cashmere blankets." He shook his head. "It was a massacre."

Valkyrie closed her eyes. "You will never not be weird."

"So how are these Apocalypse Kings going to destroy the world?" Skulduggery asked, taking the next right.

They'd done a loop, and were arriving back at the school.

Adedayo winced. "I didn't get a chance to find out before I had to leave the, uh, the swimming pool of knowledge that I mentioned. Sorry."

"And how much time do we have?"

"Not long. All they have to do is get their strength back. They're going to be feeding on souls. They're going to, like, attach themselves, I suppose, to people and they'll feed until they're strong again. They don't need to be as strong as they once were, just strong enough to do whatever it is they're gonna do. But I think I know how to beat them."

The car pulled up outside the school, and Skulduggery tilted his head. "Something you saw in their minds, while you were paddling around in the swimming pool of knowledge? A weakness?"

"Not exactly," said Adedayo, and cleared his throat. "*Má ṣi àpótí.*"

"What's that?" Valkyrie asked.

"It's the last thing *Ìyá Agba* said to me. I think it's a spell. I think, maybe, it'll stop them, or maybe trap them in the box again. *Àpótí* means *box*, I think."

"A spell, eh?" Valkyrie said, looking doubtful.

"What?" said Adedayo. "Don't you do spells?"

"Not really," Skulduggery said. "Spells can be useful in focusing your intent, distilling it down to its basic and most potent essence . . . but, in general, spells aren't really a thing."

"Oh," said Adedayo. "OK." He nodded, like he was accepting what they were saying, but he still thought his grandmother's words were a spell. He still thought they could be useful. "Can you stop them?"

"That's why we're here," Skulduggery said with utmost confidence.

Relief flushed the anxiety from his bones, and Adedayo

smiled. "Thank you. Thank you." Valkyrie and Skulduggery nodded. Didn't say anything. "So, uh . . . will I just get out?"

"Yes," Skulduggery said. "That would be a splendid idea."

Valkyrie let Adedayo out on her side, then got back in. Before Adedayo could say anything else, they drove off.

He hesitated. Then waved.

6

The next morning he felt better. Valkyrie Cain and Skulduggery Pleasant were going to take care of things. They were going to stop the Apocalypse Kings and life would return to normal, and nothing bad that happened would be his fault. Adedayo could go back to focusing on the debates.

"Argue with me," said his dad at breakfast. He held up a slice of toast. "Convince me to give this piece of toast to you."

Adedayo frowned. "But that's your toast."

"This is practice. Training. Come on now. Convince me."

Adedayo nodded, frowned at the piece of toast, his mind working to come up with persuasive arguments. "Please can I have that toast?" he asked.

"No," his dad said, sighing.

"Aw," said Adedayo, "please?"

"Ade, this is not an argument. When you debate, you have to *convince*. That's the whole point of debating. Convince me to give you my toast."

"Dad?"

"Yes?"

"Give me your toast."

"Dear God," said his dad, "you are dreadful at this."

"I told you," Adedayo said, slurping his orange juice. "I told you I was really bad at debating. But everyone said I should do it."

"He's too nice," Adedayo's mum said to her husband. "That's his problem."

"Thank you, Mum," said Adedayo, "even though it sounded like an insult, the way you said it."

His mum grinned. "You're going to be late for school."

"But I haven't finished breakfast."

She took the slice of toast from her husband's hand and gave it to him. "There you go."

"Hey," his dad said.

Adedayo took a big bite. "Victory."

He was halfway to school when the big black car pulled up beside him, and Valkyrie hopped out, still wearing the school uniform, and held the door open. Adedayo didn't know what else to do, so he got in.

"What's going on?" he asked, once they started driving.

"Our psychic friends," Skulduggery said, "they tracked these Apocalypse Kings to your school."

"What?" Adedayo said, his eyes widening. "Why? Why would they go there?"

"They scanned your mind," said Valkyrie, "and your

school is somewhere you know well, with plenty of people walking around, each one fitted with a juicy little soul, ready for plucking. It makes sense that they'd choose it for a hunting ground."

Adedayo stared. "They're going after the people in my school?"

"Don't worry," Skulduggery said as they approached the school gates, "we'll be here to search for them, stop them, and keep everyone else safe." He pressed his collar-bones and a new face flowed up, one with a hooked nose and a moustache. "How's this? Is this one OK?"

"It's fine," said Valkyrie.

"Fine, but not great?"

"It'll do."

"I need it to be great. I'll be wearing it for hours."

"Then it's great."

"OK. I believe you."

They drove slowly into the school, the crowds of students parting, staring at the car as it passed.

"What, um, what's happening?" Adedayo asked. "What's going on?"

"We're going undercover," said Valkyrie. "I'll be a student, obviously, and he'll be a teacher."

"No," said Adedayo. "What? No. That's not a good idea."

"Nonsense. It's a wonderful idea," Skulduggery said, stopping in the far corner of the staff car park. Safely away from prying eyes, they got out and Skulduggery opened the boot. He placed his hat on the carved wooden box that had started this whole mess, and took out a teacher's black robe. He put it on, completing the look with a six-sided hat sporting a golden tassel. He stood there with his hands on his hips and said, "Am I not magnificent?"

Valkyrie frowned at the hat. "What's *that*?"

"It's called a tam, Valkyrie."

"You're not wearing that."

"I am, as it turns out."

"No, you're not."

"May I remind you that I'm a teacher and you're a student? Therefore, you will do as I command."

Valkyrie flicked her hand and the six-sided hat flew into her grip. She clicked the fingers of her other hand and suddenly she was holding a ball of flame. She set fire to the tam, then dropped it.

"I see," Skulduggery said slowly.

"But I don't think any of this is a good idea," said Adedayo. "I think you might, like, raise suspicions or something."

"Why would we do that?" Skulduggery asked, taking another six-sided hat from the boot and putting it on.

"Because you don't seem to be very good at keeping a low profile."

Shadows leaped from Valkyrie's ring and slashed the tam from Skulduggery's head.

"We are excellent at keeping a low profile," she muttered. "Skulduggery, don't you dare put on another—"

He put on another, the tassel dangling in front of his face.

Valkyrie glared. "How many of those do you have?"

"Eight," he said.

"And you're aware that they're ridiculous and they make you look stupid?"

"I am aware that they are amazing and they make me look like a teacher."

"No teacher wears any of that stuff any more."

"Then I will usher in a revival of the trend."

She glowered. "Fine. You want to look stupid, you go ahead and look stupid."

"Thank you, I will."

"Will you even be allowed into the school building?" Adedayo asked.

Skulduggery shut the boot and locked the car. "Don't you worry, Adedayo. As far as the faculty is aware, I am a substitute teacher filling in for an absent member of staff, and Valkyrie has just transferred here. Most of the necessary paperwork has already been forged."

"Most?"

Skulduggery adjusted his tassel, and grinned. "Quite. Most is all you need, most of the time. And, for those times when most isn't enough, unswerving confidence is bound to see you through. Come now. We have a world to save."

7

Adedayo took his seat in Irish class and waited for the room to fill up. Valkyrie was the last one in, and Miss Coll tapped her ruler on the desk to call for silence.

"We have a new student joining us today," she announced. "Valerie, is it? Valerie, welcome. Most teachers would embarrass you by making you stand up and tell us a bit about yourself, but I've always found that to be needlessly cruel, so stand up and tell us a bit about yourself, there's a good girl."

It seemed to Adedayo that there wasn't a whole lot that could embarrass a girl like Valkyrie, and she stood there like she was standing in her own living room.

"Right," she said, "yes. Hi, everyone. I'm Valerie. A few of you might know me from my appearance in maths class yesterday. Like I said, I'm something of a prodigy, something of a genius, but I'm modest, and I hate showing off, so don't ask me to prove it in any way. I don't know anyone here apart from Adedayo, so I'd appreciate it if I could sit next to him just until I get settled. Because of how shy I am." She fixed Massoud with a look. "I'll take your desk, if you don't mind."

Massoud blinked at her for a moment, then looked round the room for support. When he received none, he sighed, gathered his stuff and moved to the empty desk at the front of the class.

"Cheers," Valkyrie said. "Also I don't have my books yet, so I'll have to share." She moved the desk closer to Adedayo's, and sat.

Miss Coll looked at her. "You're quite an assertive young lady, aren't you?"

Valkyrie raised an eyebrow. "Am I?"

The lesson began, the class splitting up into pairs to hold conversations in the Irish language.

"What are we meant to be looking for?" Adedayo whispered. "The Kings won't be just walking around out in the open, will they?"

"Wouldn't that be nice?" Valkyrie responded. "Oh, that would make our job so much easier. But no, they'll probably disguise themselves, so we'll have to stay alert for something out of place. We don't know how these guys are gonna do what they need to do, so just keep your eyes open, you know?"

"Eyes open," Adedayo repeated, looking round the room. "Right."

"And we can't discount the possibility of possession."

He looked back at her. "I'm sorry, what?"

"Possession," Valkyrie said again. "When these Apocalypse

Kings choose a target, there's the possibility that, in order to feed on the soul, they might have to possess that person."

"Like, *possess* possess? Like control their actions?"

"I might be wrong, but it's something to look out for."

"Have . . . have you ever been possessed?"

"Not me personally, but I know people who have. It's not nice. Even after it's over, you feel rotten, apparently. People like us, we'd recover a lot faster than mortals, but even so . . . Does not sound like a good time to me."

"So anyone in this school could be possessed right now?"

"It's a possibility." She sighed. "This whole thing is totally unfair, to be honest."

"What do you mean?"

Valkyrie gave a quiet grunt. "The Faceless Ones may have been a threat way back when, but the last time they tried to break through into this reality we pushed them out again. So the Apocalypse Kings want to destroy the world to starve the Faceless Ones . . . but there *aren't* any Faceless Ones to *starve*. They came, they saw, we conquered."

"Do you think the Apocalypse Kings will realise that?"

"I doubt it. They've been in that box since long before recorded history, and the only thing they've had to focus on has been the destruction of every living being on the planet. I don't think they'll be changing their minds any time soon."

"Good point."

"Make sure," Miss Coll announced loudly, "that whatever it is you're talking about it is *as Gaeilge*, yes? *In Irish*. That's the whole point of the class, after all."

She raised an eyebrow at Adedayo and Valkyrie, and Adedayo frowned back suspiciously.

After Irish, it was history. Once again, Valkyrie sat beside Adedayo as his classmates chatted and laughed among themselves. The teacher was late. A feeling of cold dread overtook Adedayo.

And then Skulduggery swept into the room, his robe billowing behind him like a cape caught in a crosswind. The class went quiet.

"Oh dear," Valkyrie muttered.

8

Skulduggery got to his chair, frowned at it, and looked up. His moustache twitched, like it was about to bolt from his face.

Niall put up his hand.

"Aha!" said Skulduggery. "A question already! Yes, young sir? What do you have burning inside you, curiosity-wise?"

"Why are you wearing gloves?"

"I have cold hands," Skulduggery answered.

Clodagh leaned forward in her seat. "Why are you wearing that hat?"

"It keeps my head warm."

"Why are you wearing a cloak?" asked Bolanle.

"It billows impressively when I walk."

Seimi folded his arms. "What's with the moustache?"

Skulduggery tilted his head. "I have a moustache?"

The students stared.

"Welcome," Skulduggery said loudly, "to this class of –" he looked at the books on his desk – "history. Ah, excellent. That's one of my specialist subjects, you know, as I was there for most of it. My name is Mister Me. You may call me 'sir' or 'Your Lordship'."

"Your name is Me?" Cian asked.

"Yes."

"The *word* Me?"

"The *name* Me, actually, but yes."

"That's not a name."

"Yes, it is. It's mine. I happen to come from a long line of reluctant narcissists. We don't like to talk about it."

"So . . . so *you* are *Me*."

There were a few laughs, and Skulduggery took a moment, then broke into an unnervingly huge grin. "Ah! I get it! Yes! Wonderful! You, boy, have a keen wit! I shall call you Barnaby!"

"That's not my name."

Skulduggery waved away the objection. "I have neither the time nor the inclination to learn names – and that goes for all of you – so I will call you by whatever pops into my head. Try not to be offended by my casual indifference to your feelings – we'll get on so much better if you can manage that. Now then, as a class, what topic are you studying right now?"

"Uh," Rafaela said, "we're revising the Great Famine."

"Ah, the Great Famine!" Skulduggery repeated. "Thank you, Winifred! Also called the Great Hunger or the Great Starvation – *great* as in widespread, not *great* as in wonderful. Caused by what? Can anybody tell me?"

Caitlyn raised a hand. "Potato blight."

"Potato blight," Skulduggery said, "yes! The dreaded *Phytophthora infestans* that swept across Europe in 1845 had a particularly devastating effect on Ireland because . . . why . . .?"

"Because people loved potatoes," said Raunak, and everybody laughed.

"Did they, though?" Skulduggery asked. He perched on the edge of his desk, adjusted his tassel, and observed the class grimly. "Let me tell you a story, then, of a nation forced to export huge quantities of livestock, fish, beans, peas – even honey – to Britain while being left with nothing but fields of rotting potatoes for themselves. Let me tell you a story of pain, of prejudice, of cruelty and of sacrifice. Let me tell you a story of people. A story of . . . yes?"

Haley lowered her hand. "Mister Me—"

"Please," Skulduggery said, "call me Your Lordship."

She sighed. "Your Lordship, we have our notes, and a test at the end of the week. We really don't need stories of people."

"But that's what history is!" Skulduggery exclaimed. "History isn't a list of dates or a collection of events – history is people. It's the decisions they make, and the consequences of those decisions. History is a jigsaw puzzle, and when you have all the pieces in place you can step back and finally see the whole picture laid out before you. History is a mystery waiting to be solved."

Rania held up her textbook. "Mystery solved, sir."

"Ha!" Skulduggery barked so loudly that Adedayo actually jumped. "You can't get history from a textbook! You can't find truth in a Contents page! History is a living, breathing thing!"

"Hold on," said Conor. "So history is people, a jigsaw puzzle, a mystery, *and* it's a living, breathing thing?"

"It's all of these things and more," Skulduggery said, "and it's a mistake to think that it can be captured and placed into a safe little cage on a safe little page to be memorised. History defies your tests and it denies your exams. But they don't want you to know that."

"Who?" asked Lucy. "Who doesn't want us to know?"

"Governments," Skulduggery said, almost whispering. "Corporations. Textbook manufacturers. They're all in on it. That's why I could never be a teacher – the idea that I'd be regurgitating falsehood upon falsehood for generation after generation would be, frankly, more than I could handle."

"What do you mean, you could never be a teacher?" Cian said. "You *are* a teacher."

"Once again, Barnaby, your quick wits impress me. Have a gold star." Skulduggery dug into a pocket in his robe and flung a fistful of tiny gold stars across the room.

"Uh, thank you," said Cian, brushing them from his hair.

9

Ian Tynan had been a teacher at the school for eighteen years, and he was proud of the fact that he made time to chat to each and every substitute teacher who passed through those hallowed doors, no matter how short a time they were here for. The new guy, the one called Me, was a tall one, with an interesting moustache, and he wore a robe and one of those six-sided hats. He stood in the middle of the staffroom, peering at every teacher who passed.

Ian walked up to him. "Welcome to the madhouse," he chuckled. "Name's Ian."

They shook hands. "Hello, Ian. The name's Me. Honolulu Me."

Ian frowned slightly. "That's quite an unusual name you got there."

"And yet believable," said Honolulu. "My parents met in Hawaii, you see. It's where they fell in love. After a whirlwind romance, they got married, and I was born nine months later, which you'll find is the customary length of time for a pregnancy to come to full term. They named me Honolulu, after the city that changed their lives. This is not an unusual decision, as many people are named after geographical locations."

"That's actually very sweet."

"Is it?" said Honolulu. "Good. They died soon after in a terrible parasailing accident."

"Oh. Oh, no. They were sharing the same parasail when it . . .?"

"No, actually, they were on separate parasail wings, as they're called, but the boats that were towing them passed too close to each other and, well, I'm sure you can imagine what happened next. Still, at least they died in each other's arms."

"That's . . . awful."

"After their sad demise, I was raised in a series of orphanages, in which I had many adventures, and eventually I grew up and became a teacher. That's the story of my life. Do you have a story of your life, Ian?"

"Not . . . not one as eventful as yours."

"Then I thank you for not sharing it with me. Can I ask you a question, though? Have you noticed anything unusual lately?"

"What kind of unusual?"

Honolulu chuckled. "Oh, nothing sinister, I assure you! Just regular levels of unusual. Have you noticed, for instance, somebody acting strangely, or someone seeming drained of energy, or maybe you've seen some ghostly apparitions, anything like that?"

"Apparitions?"

"Ghostly apparitions, yes. What about voices? Have you been hearing any voices?"

"You mean apart from yours? No, no voices."

"Oh, good," said Honolulu, failing to hide the look of disappointment on his face.

"You're a strange man, Honolulu."

"It's a strange world, Ian."

10

Alesha Walsh had been a student at the school for three years, but she remembered quite clearly the feeling of walking in and not knowing anyone, so, when she saw the new girl sitting alone in the cafeteria, she walked over and sat next to her.

"Hi," she said. "I'm Alesha. You're Valerie, right?"

"Yes," the new girl said, smiling. "Hey there."

"Just to let you know, everyone's having a big discussion about why you're switching schools in the middle of term. Some of my friends reckon you got kicked out of your last school for fighting, while others reckon you just burned it to the ground. Are either of those close to the truth?"

"Not especially," Valerie said. "My folks got new jobs and we had to move – that's the entire story. Sorry to disappoint."

"I'm sure they'll get over it," Alesha said, and smiled again. "This place isn't so bad. You've got your different groups that you need to be aware of, though." She nodded to a table in front of them. "Those are the sporty types, the jocks, as the Americans would say, although they're not really that sporty, all things considered, and they do have plenty of other interests."

She indicated a table next to one of the windows. "Over there, you have the geeks, and all they ever talk about are comics and movies and books, but they're quite well liked because everyone loves that stuff."

She pointed again. "There you have your popular girls, the pretty ones. Some of them are really nice, and, while there are a few who aren't classically beautiful, everyone's welcome, you know?" She scanned the room. "After that, there are the weirdos, the burnouts and the losers, but they tend to mingle with all the other groups because everyone has redeeming qualities and no one is left out. And I think that's it, really."

"And where does Adedayo fit into all this?"

"Oh. To be honest, I'm not too sure. He's not the *best* at sports, and he's not *amazingly* geeky, and he doesn't get the *best* grades, but, um . . . oh! He's a member of the debating club, did you know that?"

"I didn't."

"I mean, yeah, I'd say he's quite a reluctant member, if you know what I mean? He doesn't really like arguing all that much, which is a drawback. But he's cute and he's nice and he's just the right kind of weird, so if you fancy him, I say go for it."

"I'll keep that in mind," Valerie said, smiling. "It sounds like a nice school."

Alesha shrugged. "Ah, it has its problems, the same as everywhere. You get bullies, and you get people being mean to each other, and you get those who just can't seem to fit in . . . but, on the whole, it's not bad."

"And you're the welcoming committee, are you?"

"Ha! Hardly. I just thought you could use some company."

"Well, that's very nice of you."

"I'll introduce you around and you'll make friends in no time, just you see."

A girl went past their table, her head down. "Hey, Lorna, come say hello! Lorna? Lorna!" But Lorna just kept walking, and Alesha rolled her eyes. "OK, that wasn't the best example, but everyone else is lovely, I swear!"

Valerie grinned. "I'll take your word for it."

11

Debating practice went disastrously, as it usually did. Adedayo was given the task of arguing against the idea that society should eat the rich, but ended up persuading everyone – himself included – that eating the rich would probably be a good idea, all things considered.

The bell sounded, the corridors filled with students heading to their next class, and Adedayo rushed for the toilet. He got halfway there when Valkyrie appeared at his elbow.

"Who are you following?" she asked, peering ahead of them.

"What?"

"Who's your suspect?"

"I don't have one."

"Then why are you sneaking around?"

"I'm not sneaking," said Adedayo. "That's just how I walk when I'm bursting to go to the loo."

"Oh." He squeezed through the throng. She barged through after him. "What's your next class?"

"Chemistry," he said.

She made a face. "I hate chemistry."

"But, like I said, I have to go to the toilet now."

"Cool," she said, still at his elbow.

"You can't follow me in there."

"Sorry? Oh! Yeah, of course. Duh."

He went to walk off, then turned. "What happens if we don't find the Apocalypse Kings before the final bell?"

"Then we start again tomorrow."

"And do you think, um, Mister Me will come back? It's just, I don't feel he's blending in as well as he thinks he is."

They watched Skulduggery march down the corridor, smiling at nothing.

"Yeah," Valkyrie said, "he's pretty awful at it. It's been so long since he was, y'know, alive, that he's completely forgotten how to act around normal people. I'm much better at it."

"Yeah," Adedayo muttered.

She looked at him sharply. "What?"

"Sorry?"

"You said *yeah* like you didn't mean it. You don't think I'm blending in?"

"I don't know. I suppose it kinda depends on your definition of blending in."

"I'm a sixteen-year-old blending in with a bunch of other sixteen-year-olds. I can't *not* blend in. That's like saying a blade of grass isn't blending in with the rest of the lawn. Why do you think I'm not blending in?"

Adedayo chose his words carefully. "You're very confident."

"So?"

"Most people aren't that confident – especially when you're the new kid."

"But this is how I've always been."

"Oh. OK. Is this what you're like in your own school? Do you even still go to school?"

"Of course I do," Valkyrie said. Then shrugged one shoulder. "Well, technically, it's not me."

"I'm not sure I understand."

The corridor was emptying fast so she lowered her voice. "Technically, it's my reflection. It steps out of the mirror and goes to school in my place and does my homework and spends time with my family, stuff like that. It means I'm not missing out on anything."

"You have a magical reflection? And it takes over your life?"

"Only the boring bits."

"I'm not really sure how to, like, process that."

"*You* can have a magical reflection too, you know."

"Seriously? So I could, like, send it in to do my exams and stuff?"

"Magic, dude. It's awesome."

Her phone beeped, and Adedayo swallowed the urge to tell her that they weren't allowed to have their phones on during school hours.

"Elliot," she said, looking at the screen. "Skulduggery suspects a teacher called Elliot."

"This way," said Adedayo, and Valkyrie followed him. They got to Mr Elliot's classroom. The door was still open and they watched him sitting at his desk, his shoulders hunched, staring into space and completely ignoring the students.

"Is this normal behaviour from him?" Valkyrie asked, keeping her voice low.

"Not really," Adedayo answered. "He doesn't look well."

"Having a hungry god leech off your soul will do that to you, I suppose." She took Adedayo's arm and moved them on. "OK, so we have our first suspect. Now we need two more."

"Cool," said Adedayo. "But you head on to chemistry, OK? I'll meet you there."

Valkyrie frowned. "Where are you going?"

He went to answer and she clicked her fingers.

"Toilet! Yes! Go! Pee! Pee and be free!"

She walked off and Adedayo shook his head. She was so weird.

He hurried on. A couple of boys were at the urinals so he stepped into one of the cubicles. He heard the boys leave and then he finished up, flushed the toilet, and stepped out.

Lorna stood at a washbasin, staring at her reflection in the mirror. She was pale. Her spine curved.

"Lorna?" Adedayo said. "Everything OK?"

She turned suddenly, smiling. "Yes," she said brightly. "Everything's great. How are you, Adedayo?"

"I'm, uh, I'm good. Lorna, these are the boys' toilets."

She blinked. "Oh," she said. "Oh dear."

There was a flash, like a light bulb flaring, and in that instant Adedayo saw the hazy figure of the Cythraul looming behind Lorna, his tentacles stuck in her head. Then he was gone again, almost immediately.

"I should get to class," Adedayo said.

"Oh dear," Lorna said again. "You saw, didn't you? Oh dear, oh dear. What *are* we going to do about that?"

Her smile widened.

12

Adedayo bolted, but she was on him before he reached the door, and she tossed him behind her like he was nothing but an old coat. He somehow managed to keep upright as he bounced off the wall, stumbling into the cubicle.

"You saw me," Lorna said.

He slammed the cubicle door. Locked it. The latch rattled loosely. "No, I didn't!" he called.

"You saw me," Lorna sang. "That's a pity. We were going to leave you alone. We thought it polite. You're the one who set us free, after all. The least we can do is refrain from eating your soul."

Adedayo pressed his hands against the door. "I won't tell anyone, I promise."

Through the gap between the hinges, he watched her shape get closer. "I know," she said.

She shoved the door and it was like a truck hit it, flinging Adedayo back. He scrambled on to the toilet seat as she reached for him and vaulted clumsily over the cubicle wall. He hit the ground and bolted as she lunged, grabbing the back of his jumper. He turned, twisted, pulling his head and arms free, and then he was sprinting into the corridor.

She came after him.

Adedayo ran, adrenaline pumping through his system, painfully aware of how close she was, of how her finger-tips grasped at the shirt on his back. Up the stairs, turning right, running alongside the balcony that overlooked the sports hall. She was going to get him. He was going to slow down or trip or make a mistake and then she was going to have him and this time there'd be no escape. He knew it. It was inevitable. He was dead unless he did something unexpected.

He launched himself over the balcony and Lorna screeched and grabbed his wrist and he swung back and hit the wall, but her grip wasn't good and she had to let him go and he fell, slamming down on to the soles of his feet, jarring his knees, teeth crunching together, and then he was spinning, running on shaking legs, bursting through the double doors into the sunlight.

"Adedayo!" Valkyrie yelled from the Old House, and Adedayo sprinted across the courtyard. She grabbed him. "Let's go," she said, bolting for the stairs. "Skulduggery's waiting. We have a plan."

"What kind of plan?" Adedayo gasped, trying to keep up.

"A good one," she said. "Well, kinda."

He glanced back as the door burst open. Lorna stormed in, looked up, right at him, and smiled.

Adedayo tripped over the top step, would have fallen if Valkyrie hadn't kept him upright, turning him to the second set of stairs. She stopped suddenly and he crashed into her. Mr Elliot stood halfway up, the hazy image of the Sathariel looming over him.

"Hold on," Valkyrie whispered, wrapping an arm round Adedayo's waist. She brought her other arm in and it was like the air seized them and flung them high over Elliot's head.

A small part of Adedayo's fear-spiked mind recognised how exhilarating it all was.

They crashed on to the landing and Valkyrie led the way onwards, to a part of the Old House Adedayo had never been. Down a narrow corridor they went, up some steps, turning a corner, up more steps, before arriving in an attic space the size of a swimming pool. The room was clean and empty, the ceiling high, the windows flooding it with light.

"So what's the plan?" Adedayo asked, trying to get his breath back. "Where's Skulduggery?"

"He's supposed to be here," Valkyrie said, frowning.

Adedayo kept his eyes on the door. "Maybe you should call him? Maybe you should call him now, like? It's a bit of an emergency, don't you think? Lorna said – or, no, the Cythraul controlling her said – they were going to eat my soul."

"They're *not* going to eat your soul," Valkyrie said firmly.

"He said they weren't planning on it, out of politeness, but he's changed his mind and he's gonna eat it."

"He said that, did he?"

"He did."

"Well, I can assure you, Adedayo, we are *not* going to eat your soul."

Adedayo stopped moving for a few seconds, and then he turned, ever so slowly. Valkyrie stood there, smiling calmly, while the Deathless stood behind her, his fingers inside her head.

13

"Oh dear," said Lorna, joining them in the attic, Elliot at her heels.

Adedayo backed up against one wall, keeping all three of the Apocalypse Kings in sight. "How long?" he asked.

Valkyrie's smile widened. "How long have I been controlling her? Only a few minutes. I had attached myself to one of your school friends but, once I sensed Valkyrie's sheer power, I couldn't resist the – what's the word? – *upgrade*."

"We should eat their souls," Lorna said.

"We agreed that we would keep the damage we inflict to a minimum," Valkyrie responded. Her face, her voice, his words. "When they are dead, they will need their souls to move through to what comes next."

Elliot nodded. "We will feed but not devour. It is what we agreed."

"But that was before," said Lorna. "You can feel it as I can. It will be better for us if we consume their souls completely. It will make us stronger."

"This isn't about strength," Valkyrie said. "This is about punishing the Faceless Ones. And we are strong enough already – it is time to stand on our own."

"I agree," said Elliot.

Valkyrie stiffened, and the Deathless stepped away from her, letting her collapse. He stood there, clenching and unclenching his fists, rolling his shoulders, working his jaw – getting used to having his own flesh-and-blood body once more.

Mr Elliot grunted and then sank to the floor, as unconscious as he was ungraceful, and the Sathariel stood over him, his hand going to his brow as if the light was hurting his eyes behind his veil.

"I object to this," Lorna said.

"I know," the Deathless replied.

She arched her back and gritted her teeth, and her knees gave out and she fell – but the Cythraul caught her, and lowered her gently to the ground.

"This isn't right," Adedayo said softly.

"You will be treated fairly," the Deathless said. "You have my word."

"Well, you're planning on killing everyone, so right now your word doesn't mean much to me, no offence."

"The Deathless sit in judgement," said the Cythraul.

"The Deathless do not lie," said the Sathariel.

"I would not mislead you, Adedayo," the Deathless said. "The other races, the Faceless Ones among them, relied on my kind to be impartial, to be just. We even had the confidence of Those Who Slumber, Whose Name We Dare Not Speak Lest They Rouse to Waking. But that was before the Scourge, before the Great Betrayal."

Adedayo frowned. "I recognise some of what you're saying. Those Who Slumber, Whose Name We Dare Not Speak Lest They Rouse to Waking. They were in your mind when I looked into it, in the swimming pool of knowledge, but . . ."

"But I hid the details from you," said the Deathless, "as I hid so much else. There are truths you are not ready for – truths that would harm you and tear you in two."

"How very considerate of you," said Skulduggery, walking in. His teacher's robe and six-sided hat were gone – as was his face. He was just a skeleton now, and he wore his other hat, the one that went with his suit, dipped low over one eye socket. "So what is it going to be?"

The Deathless turned to him. "I beg your pardon?"

"How are you going to do it? How are you going to kill everyone? Plague? Pestilence? Are you going to snap your fingers and we'll all crumble to dust?"

"No," the Deathless said. "We're going to die."

"I see," Skulduggery said slowly.

Valkyrie sat up, blinking. Mr Elliot and Lorna – mere mortals, without the benefit of magic in their blood – stayed unconscious.

"Our passing will cause our souls to reverberate," said the Cythraul, "and those reverberations will shake this world to pieces."

The Sathariel continued. "The ground will quake and the mountains will tumble. Fire will rain from the skies and the seas shall boil and reclaim the land."

Skulduggery nodded. "So, bring your umbrella is what you're saying."

"*Can* you even die?" Valkyrie asked the Deathless as she stood.

"Do not allow our name to mislead you, Valkyrie. In our arrogance, my kind named ourselves, for we thought there existed no power that could rob us of life. We were, as in a great many things, wrong. By the time the Faceless Ones betrayed us all, we had already been thoroughly humbled." He smiled. "But the name stuck."

"They're not here," said Adedayo. "The Faceless Ones. You're doing this because of them, because of what they did to your race, but they're not even around any more. They've been banished."

"Yet this world reeks of them," said the Sathariel. "The air has grown stale with the stench of them. They have made their mark here and they wish to return."

"They see this place as their rightful home," the Cythraul said. "While they still live, they will seek to cross realities until they are worshipped here once again. But, when they arrive, we want them to set foot on the remnants of a barren land – a land devoid of humanity."

"Then how about you help us?" Valkyrie said. "How about, instead of spoiling their home, you stand by our side if they ever come back?"

"There are but three of us," said the Cythraul, "and the Faceless Ones' numbers are immeasurable."

The Deathless shook his head. "If we fight them, we may lose, and forgo our chance at retribution. Destroying their food source, however, destroying their homeland . . . that is guaranteed to inflict damage."

"Fair enough," said Valkyrie. "I mean, if you're happy with merely *damaging* the Faceless Ones, instead of actually fighting and possibly destroying them, then hey, you do you."

"You will not change our minds."

"Nope. Looks like you decided what you're gonna do a long time ago, and you've got no intention of changing."

"Your attempt at reverse psychology will not work."

"I don't even want it to."

"You are amusing," said the Deathless, as he took a glass ball from his robe. Energy flowed from his hand into the ball, and Adedayo watched the Deathless sag. When he was done, he handed it to the Sathariel, who took his turn.

"Let me guess," said Skulduggery. "That orb is your equivalent of loading a gun with three bullets, yes?"

The Sathariel slumped, and handed the orb to the Cythraul.

"Then what do you do?" Skulduggery continued. "It looks fragile, so I imagine you destroy it, releasing the bullets that will then seek you out?"

The Deathless smiled. "You've seen this before?"

"I've seen something like it, yes. A way to ensure you all die at the same instant."

The Cythraul handed the orb back to the Deathless. The different-coloured energies flickered around inside like fish in a bowl.

"Something to hang on the Christmas tree," said Valkyrie. "Cute."

"You won't have to wait long," said the Sathariel. "Once the orb settles, we will end your suffering."

Valkyrie rolled her shoulders. "Putting all that energy into the orb really took it out of you, didn't it? Even the way you're standing right now – you look dead on your feet. Don't you think so, Skulduggery?"

"Yes, I do," Skulduggery said.

"We are still more than strong enough to restrain you," said the Sathariel.

Skulduggery tilted his head. "You think so?"

The Sathariel raised an arm, but Skulduggery flew across the room, smashing into him.

The Cythraul moved to help, but shadows leaped from Valkyrie's ring and wrapped round him, binding his many tentacles.

The Deathless backed away from it all, then turned and ran out of the room.

"Adedayo!" Skulduggery called as he wrestled. "Stop him!"

Adedayo nodded. Then shouted, "*What?*"

The Sathariel slammed Skulduggery back against the wall.

"We can't do it!" Skulduggery yelled. He punched the Sathariel, drove a knee into his leg, followed it with an elbow shot to the face. "We're a bit busy! You'll have to!"

"But I can't use magic when I'm panicking!"

"It's not about magic!" Valkyrie cried as the Cythraul broke free of her shadows. "It's about trying your best, you muppet!"

The tentacles grabbed her, picked her up, hurled her across the room.

Adedayo hesitated – then ran after the Deathless.

14

He caught a glimpse of the Deathless turning a corner, and sprinted after him.

This was stupid. This was amazingly dumb. What did he know about fighting a god? But he had no choice. There was no one else around to do it. There was no one he could turn to for help. This had to be him. He had to try. The fate of the world depended on him. His parents, his sisters, everyone he loved depended on him.

A small set of stairs led to a door that was just swinging closed. Adedayo charged up, clicking his fingers until he had a small ball of flame in his hand. He burst out on to the roof of the Old House. The Deathless stood on the roof's edge, his back to him.

Adedayo hurled the fireball. It barely made it halfway before going out.

He tried pushing at the air, but all he could manage was a slight breeze.

The Deathless turned to him slowly. Adedayo had one chance left. One slim chance.

"*Má ṣi àpótí!*" he shouted.

The Deathless raised an eyebrow. "Pardon?"

Adedayo frowned, wondering if he'd got the pronunciation wrong. "*Má ṣi àpótí,*" he repeated, a lot quieter this time.

The Deathless didn't react. The spell didn't work.

Adedayo realised his fists were clenched. He unclenched them. "Please don't do it," he said.

The Deathless gazed at the orb in his hand. "I promise you, what awaits your soul in death is far greater than what this life has had to offer you."

"Maybe it is, but I don't want that yet. Barely anyone does. You're robbing us, all of us, all of humanity, of who we are."

"Who you are is wonderful," said the Deathless, looking at him, "but ultimately unimportant. Your soul is eternal, Adedayo, or as close to eternal as can be. By contrast, you, your memories, your personality – these things exist for so brief a time that it could be argued they don't exist at all."

Adedayo took a step forward. "But they exist *now*. I exist now. I'm right here. I'm talking to you. I'm asking you not to destroy us."

The orb started to pulse with a soft glow. "It is ready," said the Deathless. "It is time."

"Wait! Please wait! I get that you think I'm unimportant, that humanity is unimportant, but who are you to decide this?"

"I'm a god," said the Deathless.

That was, admittedly, a good point. "OK, right, you're a god, so I'm asking you to be a merciful god. You want to destroy the Faceless Ones because they wiped out your race. But what are you about to do? You're going to kill my race the same way the Faceless Ones killed yours."

"I am fully aware of the hypocrisy of my stance."

"Then be better than them. Isn't that the least you can do, after what happened? Isn't that how you defeat them?"

"We are under no illusion, Adedayo. We have long since lost this battle." He raised his hand, preparing to hurl the orb to the ground.

"Not yet you haven't," Adedayo said quickly. "Not while you're still alive. Yeah, they murdered your race, they murdered the Cythraul's race and the Sathariel's race – but they couldn't kill you, could they? They could only trap you. You know what that says to me? It says they're scared. It says they feared you getting out. And now what? Now that you're out, instead of fighting them, you're going to end yourselves to spoil their food source? I don't know anything about what's out there on other planets or in other dimensions – but what's to stop the Faceless Ones from finding another world full of worshippers with souls they can eat?"

The Deathless hesitated. "This is still their home."

"So you're going to ruin it just to spite them?"

"I don't expect you to understand."

"But if you can't make me understand, maybe that's

not a fault with me. Maybe that's a fault with your argument."

The Deathless said nothing.

"I don't know what the best thing to do is, but Skulduggery and Valkyrie, and other sorcerers like them, I'm sure they'll have plans. You don't have to be the bad guys here. You could be the heroes. You could do your races proud."

"You are a good boy, Adedayo. A good human. It is a pity it has come to this."

"But I'm not alone," Adedayo responded. "I'm not the only one. The human race, we have our problems, we do, but there are plenty more good people in this world than there are bad. Give us a chance, please."

"A chance to do what? To poison your planet further? To kill yourselves your own way?"

"At least give us the chance to decide our own fate – a chance the Deathless were never given."

"You are trying to convince me that humanity is worth sparing – even though I have already looked inside your mind. I know about their petty cruelties."

"You can't judge us by the idiots, though. Judge us by the nice people. That's what you do, isn't it? Sit in judgement? All those other gods, they trusted your kind to be fair. That's all I'm asking now. Just be fair."

"This accord between my kind, the Cythrauls, and the Sathariels has long been in motion."

"That doesn't mean you have to see it through. You can

change your mind. You can focus on helping us instead of hurting us. The Faceless Ones are still out there somewhere. Don't you want to fight back? I know you do. You can deny it, if that makes you feel better, but I saw it when you let me look inside your mind. You want to fight. Not like we fight, not like humans fight, but you want to . . ." He searched for the right words. "You want to be better than them. You want to prove that you're better than them. And for you that doesn't mean beating them physically. It doesn't even mean ruining their home. It simply means that you beat them by being better than they are. You could do what you're planning to do. I can't stop you. But it's just . . . it's revenge. That's all it is."

"Revenge," said the Deathless, "is all we have left."

"That's not true, though. You've got so much more because you *are* so much more. You're talking to me. You're hearing my side of the argument. The Faceless Ones wouldn't listen to a word I said – but you're not them. You're listening. You *are* better than they are. Or, at least . . . you can be. But taking revenge on someone, on anyone, that just brings you even with them, doesn't it? It means you're operating on the same level."

The Deathless raised an eyebrow slightly. "And you want us to operate on a higher level?"

"I do. And so do you, I think. You could have the revenge that you planned, right now, by smashing that orb thing. Or you could choose not to. You could pass over it. You could let it go. And be better than them."

The Deathless smiled sadly. "You are wise, Adedayo Akinde."

"I am?"

"I will consider your words. If I decide that you are right, then we will return to our confinement. It was, if nothing else, peaceful in there. If, however, I decide that I am more right than you, that our plan is truly the way to proceed, then I hope your death is swift and painless."

Adedayo hesitated. "Cool."

The Deathless inclined his head ever so slightly, and Adedayo fainted.

15

Adedayo opened his eyes.

It was dark. Oh, God, he'd failed. He'd failed and the Apocalypse Kings had destroyed everything and everyone was dead and the world was in darkness all because of him and his stupidity and his . . . no, wait – it was night.

He was lying on the roof of the Old House, and it was night-time. Yes. That made sense.

"There you are."

He sat up as Skulduggery walked out on to the roof. "What happened?"

"You did it," Skulduggery said. "The Deathless came back down and the fighting stopped. He explained to the other two what you talked about up here and made them understand. They're quite a reasonable bunch – for gods, I mean. They abandoned their plan, retrieved their energies from the orb, and agreed to return to the box until they decide what to do with themselves. We can't lock it like the Faceless Ones did, but when you're dealing with beings like the Apocalypse Kings, you take what you can get." He stood beside him. "Well done."

"Thank you," Adedayo said, getting up. "How long have I been out here?"

"About five hours."

"Oh." His eyes widened. "My parents are going to kill me!"

"Probably."

"What about Lorna? And Mr Elliot?"

"Both fine," said Skulduggery. "They're mortals, so they won't remember anything about what happened. That's always best, I find. Things like this tend to traumatise mortal minds."

"You found him," Valkyrie said, walking on to the roof. She was wearing all black. "Wow, it's chilly up here."

Adedayo suddenly realised how cold he was, and crossed his arms. Valkyrie slipped off her jacket and handed it over.

"Go on," she said. "Until you warm up."

He accepted it gratefully.

"This is a moment, Adedayo," Skulduggery said. "In life we are offered so very few moments to truly savour – so, when they occur, you must take the opportunity to sear them into your memory. This would be, I imagine, your first time saving the world?"

"I saved the world?"

"We all did, which means the three of us can say both *We saved the world* and *I saved the world*. Go ahead. Say it."

"Uh . . ."

"Don't be shy."

Adedayo cleared his throat. "I saved the world."

"Yes, you did," said Skulduggery. "I want you to stand here on this rooftop, Adedayo, and reflect on those words. Do you know what makes a hero?"

"Bravery," said Adedayo. "Or . . . maybe fear. You can't be brave unless you're feeling scared, right? So bravery in spite of fear? Is that what makes a hero?"

Skulduggery shrugged. "I was going to say *punching*, but sure, yours is OK too."

"What do I do now? Like, do I go back to my normal life and forget about all this, or do I abandon my normal life and focus on learning magic?"

Skulduggery took a moment before answering. "I don't care," he said.

"Oh," said Adedayo.

"It's up to you," Valkyrie said. "Skulduggery can't tell you what to do. It wouldn't be right."

"And also I genuinely don't care," Skulduggery said.

Valkyrie ignored him. "When I found out about magic, that was it for me, I couldn't let it go. I wasn't about to return to my old life, not after what I'd seen – but everyone's different. Do you like your life?"

"I mean . . . I suppose."

"Do you ever feel as if something's missing?"

He was quiet for a bit. "Not before now."

"It's up to you, dude. You get involved in magic, and

it can be really, really dangerous. You could get killed doing this."

"Or you could get killed in your bedroom playing video games," Skulduggery said. "A meteor could come through your window and take your head clean off. I've seen it happen."

"You have not," Valkyrie said crossly.

"Yes, I have."

She folded her arms. "You've seen a meteor take someone's head off in their bedroom, have you?"

"Maybe not *exactly* that," he responded, somewhat grudgingly. "OK, fine, it wasn't a bedroom, it was a kitchen, and it wasn't a meteor, it was a rock, and it didn't take their head off, but it left a bruise."

"Skulduggery, did you throw a stone at someone while they were standing in their kitchen?"

"I did, yes."

She sighed, and turned her attention back to Adedayo. "It's your choice. I'm gonna leave a number with you for a place called the Sanctuary. If you decide you want to explore magic, they'll be able to help. Oh, and take a name, all right? If you become a sorcerer, you'll need a new name."

"OK," said Adedayo. "Sure. What name should I take?"

Valkyrie smiled. "I can't tell you that. If you decide to learn magic, if you're capable of putting in the work and the practice, you'll be a new person. You've just got to decide what this new person will be called."

Skulduggery checked his pocket watch. "And now we must be off. I have a tailor friend who has a new suit waiting for me to pick up, and he gets unreasonably grumpy when I'm late." He stepped right to the edge of the roof and turned. "Adedayo, it's been a pleasure working with you. Maybe we'll do it again sometime. Maybe not."

He let himself fall backwards off the edge, and disappeared.

"What a show-off," Valkyrie muttered.

Adedayo passed her back her jacket and shadows flowed from her ring, enveloping her. "See you around," she said, and, when the shadows dispersed she was gone, and Adedayo was alone on the rooftop.

16

Adedayo got home and apologised for being so late. He told his parents he'd been out walking, thinking about his *iyá agba*. They seemed to accept that, and let the matter drop.

His sisters arrived in the kitchen and announced that, even though *Ìyá Agba* was gone, and so a bedroom was suddenly available, they wanted to keep sharing. They announced this like they expected their request to be denied – his youngest sister's eyes were already brimming with tears. When they were told that was fine, they shrieked and hugged and hugged their parents and even hugged Adedayo, and ran back to their room.

Adedayo's dad chuckled and went into the living room.

"Mum," said Adedayo.

She was making herself a cup of tea. "Yes, sweetie?"

"What was *Ìyá Agba*'s life like? Back in Nigeria?"

His mum paused. "I'm not too sure, actually. She never talked about it all that much. She was happy, though. I know that." She smiled. "She used to tell me stories, when

I was your youngest sister's age. All kinds of stories she'd make up about people with amazing names all over Africa. People with magical powers. And in the stories she was always in the middle of the adventure. Always having fun. I miss her."

"I miss her too."

His mother's smile turned sad, and she took a packet of biscuits down from the cupboard and held it out. "Take two," she said, "and don't tell your sisters."

He took two, and she winked and carried her tea to the doorway.

"Mum," said Adedayo, "what does *má ṣi àpótí* mean?"

She frowned. "What?"

"It's just something *Ìyá Agba* said to me in hospital. What does it mean?"

"Are you sure that's what she said?"

"I mean . . . I might not be remembering it exactly right, but I think so."

His mum shrugged one shoulder. "It's just it's an odd thing to say, that's all. It means *don't open the box.*"

Adedayo looked at her, then nodded. "Yep," he said. "Makes sense."

Enjoyed this novella? Find out where the Skulduggery Pleasant story began with this extract from the first book in the series!

Stephanie's uncle Gordon is a writer of horror fiction. But when he dies and leaves her his estate, Stephanie learns that while he may have written horror, it certainly wasn't fiction.

Pursued by evil forces intent on recovering a mysterious key, Stephanie finds help from an unusual source – the wisecracking skeleton of a dead wizard.

When all hell breaks loose, it's lucky for Skulduggery that he's already dead. Though he's about to discover that being a skeleton doesn't stop you from being tortured, if the torturer is determined enough. And if there's anything Skulduggery hates, it's torture . . . Will evil win the day? Will Stephanie and Skulduggery stop bickering long enough to stop it? One thing's for sure: evil won't know what's hit it.

1

STEPHANIE

Gordon Edgley's sudden death came as a shock to everyone – not least himself. One moment he was in his study, seven words into the twenty-fifth sentence of the final chapter of his new book *And The Darkness Rained Upon Them*, and the next he was dead. *A tragic loss*, his mind echoed numbly as he slipped away.

The funeral was attended by family and acquaintances but not many friends. Gordon hadn't been a well-liked figure in the publishing world, for although the books he wrote – tales of horror and magic and wonder – regularly reared their heads in the bestseller lists, he had the disquieting habit of insulting people without realising it, then laughing at their shock. It was at Gordon's funeral, however, that Stephanie Edgley first caught sight of the gentleman in the tan overcoat.

He was standing under the shade of a large tree, away from the crowd, the coat buttoned up all the way despite the warmth of the afternoon. A scarf was wrapped around the lower half of his face and even from her position on the far side of the grave, Stephanie could make out the wild and frizzy hair that escaped from the wide brimmed hat he wore low over his gigantic sunglasses. She watched him, intrigued by his appearance. And then, like he knew he was being observed, he turned and walked back through the rows of headstones, and disappeared from sight.

After the service, Stephanie and her parents travelled back to her dead uncle's house, over a humpbacked bridge and along a narrow road that carved its way through thick woodland. The gates were heavy and grand and stood open, welcoming them into the estate. The grounds were vast and the old house itself was ridiculously big.

There was an extra door in the living room, a door disguised as a bookcase, and when she was younger Stephanie liked to think that no one else knew about this door, not even Gordon himself. It was a secret passageway, like in the stories she'd read, and she'd make up adventures about haunted houses and smuggled treasure. This secret passageway would always be her escape route, and the imaginary villains in these adventures would be dumbfounded by her sudden and mysterious disappearance. But now this door, this secret passageway, stood open, and there was a steady stream of people through it, and she was saddened that this little piece of magic had been taken from her.

Tea was served and drinks were poured and little sandwiches were passed around on silver trays, and Stephanie watched the mourners casually appraise their surroundings. The major topic of hushed conversation was the will. Gordon wasn't a man who inspired, or even demonstrated, any great affection, so no one could predict who would inherit his substantial fortune. Stephanie could see the greed seep into the watery eyes of her father's other brother, a horrible little man called Fergus, as he nodded sadly and spoke sombrely and pocketed the silverware when he thought no one was looking.

Fergus's wife was a thoroughly dislikeable, sharp-featured woman named Beryl. She drifted through the crowd, deep in unconvincing grief, prying for gossip and digging for scandal. Her daughters did their best to ignore Stephanie. Carol and

Crystal were twins, fifteen years old, and as sour and vindictive as their parents. Whereas Stephanie was dark-haired, tall, slim and strong, they were bottle-blonde, stumpy and dressed in clothes that made them bulge in all the wrong places. Apart from their brown eyes, no one would guess that the twins were related to her. She liked that. It was the only thing about them she liked. She left them to their petty glares and snide whispers, and went for a walk.

The corridors of her uncle's house were long and lined with paintings. The floor beneath Stephanie's feet was wooden, polished to a gleam, and the house smelled of age. Not musty exactly but... experienced. These walls and these floors had seen a lot in their time, and Stephanie was nothing but a faint whisper to them. Here one instant, gone the next.

Gordon had been a good uncle. Arrogant and irresponsible, yes, but also childish and enormous fun, with a light in his eyes, a glint of mischief. When everyone else was taking him seriously, Stephanie was privy to the winks and the nods and the half-smiles that he would shoot her way when they weren't looking. Even as a child she felt she understood him better than most. She liked his intelligence and his wit, and the way he didn't care what people thought of him. He'd been a good uncle to have. He'd taught her a lot.

She knew that her mother and Gordon had briefly dated ("courted", her mother had called it), but when Gordon had introduced her to his younger brother, it was love at first sight. Gordon liked to grumble that he had never got more than a peck on the cheek, but he had stepped aside graciously, and had quite happily gone on to have numerous torrid affairs with numerous beautiful women. He used to say that it had almost been a fair trade, but that he suspected he had lost out.

Stephanie climbed the staircase, pushed open the door to Gordon's study and stepped inside. The walls were filled with the framed covers from his bestsellers and shared space with all manner of awards. One entire wall was made up of shelves, jammed with books. There were biographies and historical novels and science texts and psychology tomes, and there were battered little paperbacks stuck in between. A lower shelf had magazines, literary reviews and quarterlies.

Stephanie passed the shelves which housed the first editions of Gordon's novels and approached the desk. She looked at the chair where he'd died, trying to imagine him there, how he must have slumped. And then, a voice so smooth it could have been made of velvet:

"At least he died doing what he loved."

She turned, surprised, to see the man from the funeral in the overcoat and hat standing in the doorway. The scarf was still wrapped, the sunglasses still on, the fuzzy hair still poking out. His hands were gloved.

"Yes," Stephanie said, because she couldn't think of anything else to say. "At least there's that."

"You're one of his nieces then?" the man asked. "You're not stealing anything, you're not breaking anything, so I'd guess you're Stephanie." She nodded and took the opportunity to look at him more closely. She couldn't see even the tiniest bit of his face beneath the scarf and sunglasses.

"Were you a friend of his?" she asked. He was tall, this man, tall and thin, though his coat made it difficult to judge.

"I was," he answered with a move of his head. This slight movement made her realise that the rest of his body was unnaturally still. "I've known him for years, met him outside a bar in New York when I was over there, back when he had just published his first novel."

Stephanie couldn't see anything behind the sunglasses – they were black as pitch. "Are you a writer too?"

"Me? No, I wouldn't know where to start. But I got to live out my writer fantasies through Gordon."

"You had writer fantasies?"

"Doesn't everyone?"

"I don't know. I don't think so."

"Oh. Then that would make me seem kind of odd, wouldn't it?"

"Well," Stephanie answered. "It would *help*."

"Gordon used to talk about you all the time, boast about his little niece. He was an individual of character, your uncle. It seems that you are too."

"You say that like you know me."

"Strong-willed, intelligent, sharp-tongued, doesn't suffer fools gladly... remind you of anyone?"

"Yes. Gordon."

"Interesting," said the man. "Because those are the exact words he used to describe you." His gloved fingers dipped into his waistcoat and brought out an ornate pocket watch on a delicate gold chain.

"Good luck in whatever you decide to do with your life."

"Thank you," Stephanie said, a little dumbly. "You too."

She felt the man smile, though she could see no mouth, and he turned from the doorway and left her there. Stephanie found she couldn't take her eyes off where he had been. Who was he? She hadn't even got his name.

She crossed over to the door and stepped out, wondering how he had vanished from sight so quickly. She hurried down the stairs and reached the large hall without seeing him. She opened the front door just as a big black car turned out on to the road. She watched him drive away, stayed there for a few moments, then reluctantly rejoined her extended family in the living room, just in time to see Fergus slip a silver ashtray into his breast pocket.

2

THE WILL

ife in the Edgley household was fairly uneventful. Stephanie's mother worked in a bank and her father owned a construction company, and she had no brothers or sisters, so the routine they had settled into was one of amiable convenience. But even so, there was always the voice in the back of her mind telling her that there should be more to her life than *this*, more to her life than the small coastal town of Haggard. She just couldn't figure out what that something was.

Her first year of secondary school had just come to a close

and she was looking forward to the summer break. Stephanie didn't like school. She found it difficult to get along with her classmates – not because they weren't nice people, but simply because she had nothing in common with them. And she didn't like teachers. She didn't like the way they demanded respect they hadn't earned. Stephanie had no problem doing what she was told, just so long as she was given a good reason why she should.

She had spent the first few days of the summer helping out her father, answering phones and sorting through the files in his office. Gladys, his secretary of seven years, had decided she'd had enough of the construction business and wanted to try her hand as a performance artist. Stephanie found it vaguely discomfiting whenever she passed her on the street, this forty-three-year-old woman doing a modern dance interpretation of Faust. Gladys had made herself a costume to go with the act, a costume, she said, that symbolised the internal struggle Faust was going through, and apparently she refused to be seen in public without it. Stephanie did her best to avoid catching Gladys's eye.

If Stephanie wasn't helping out in the office, she was either down at the beach, swimming, or locked in her room listening to music. She was in her room, trying to find the charger for her mobile phone, when her mother knocked on the door and stepped in. She was still dressed in the sombre clothes she had worn to the funeral, though Stephanie had tied back her long dark hair and changed into her usual jeans and trainers within two minutes of returning to the house.

"We got a call from Gordon's solicitor," her mother said, sounding a little surprised. "They want us at the reading of the will."

"Oh," Stephanie responded. "What do you think he left you?"

"Well, we'll find out tomorrow. You too, because you're coming with us."

"I am?" Stephanie said with a slight frown.

"Your name's on the list, that's all I know. We're leaving at ten, OK?"

"I'm supposed to be helping Dad in the morning."

"He called Gladys, asked her to fill in for a few hours, as a favour. She said yes, as long as she could wear the peanut suit."

They left for the solicitor's at a quarter past ten the next morning, fifteen minutes later than planned thanks to Stephanie's father's casual disregard for punctuality. He ambled through the house, looking like there was something he'd forgotten and he was just waiting for it to occur to him again. He

93

nodded and smiled whenever his wife told him to hurry up, said "Yes, absolutely," and just before he was due to join them in the car, he meandered off again, looking around with a dazed expression.

"He does this on purpose," Stephanie's mother said as they sat in the car, seatbelts on and ready to go. They watched him appear at the front door, shrug into his jacket, tuck in his shirt, go to step out, and then pause.

"He looks like he's about to sneeze," Stephanie remarked.

"No," her mother responded, "he's just thinking." She stuck her head out of the window. "Desmond, what's wrong now?"

He looked up, puzzled. "I think I'm forgetting something."

Stephanie leaned forward in the back seat, took a look at him and spoke to her mother, who nodded and stuck her head out again. "Where are your shoes, dear?"

He looked down at his socks – one brown, one navy – and his clouded expression cleared. He gave them the thumbs-up and disappeared from view.

"That man," her mother said, shaking her head. "Did you know he once lost a shopping centre?"

"He what?"

"I never told you that? It was the first big contract he got. His company did a wonderful job and he was driving his clients to see it, and he forgot where he put it. He drove around for almost an hour until he saw something he recognised. He may be a very talented engineer, but I swear, he's got the attention span of a goldfish. So unlike Gordon."

"They weren't very alike, were they?"

Her mother smiled. "It wasn't always that way. They used to do everything together. The three of them were inseparable."

"What, even Fergus?"

"Even Fergus. But when your grandmother died they all drifted apart. Gordon started mixing with a strange crowd after that."

"Strange in what way?"

"Ah, they probably just appeared strange to us," her mother said with a small laugh. "Your dad was getting started in the construction business and I was in college and we were what you might call normal. Gordon resisted being normal, and his friends, they kind of scared us. We never knew what they were into, but we knew it wasn't anything..."

"*Normal.*"

"Exactly. They scared your dad most of all though."

"Why?"

Stephanie's father walked out of the house, shoes on, and closed the front door after him.

"I think he was more like Gordon than he liked to let on," her mother said quietly, and then her dad got into the car.

"OK," he said proudly. "I'm ready."

They looked at him as he nodded, chuffed with himself. He strapped on his seatbelt and turned the key. The engine purred to life. Stephanie waved to Jasper, an eight-year-old boy with unfortunate ears, as her dad backed out on to the road, put the car in gear and they were off, narrowly missing their wheelie bin as they went.

The drive to the solicitor's office in the city took a little under an hour and they arrived twenty minutes late. They were led up a flight of creaky stairs to a small office, too warm to be comfortable, with a large window that offered a wonderful view of the brick wall across the street. Fergus and Beryl were there, and they showed their displeasure at having been kept waiting by looking at their watches and scowling. Stephanie's parents took the remaining chairs and Stephanie stood behind them as the solicitor peered at them through cracked spectacles.

"Now can we get started?" Beryl snapped.

The solicitor, a short man named Mr Fedgewick, with the girth and appearance of a sweaty bowling ball, tried smiling. "We still have one more person to wait on," he said and Fergus's eyes bulged.

"Who?" he demanded. "There can't be anyone else, we are the only siblings Gordon had. Who is it? It's not some charity, is it? I've never trusted charities. They always want something from you."

"It's, it's not a charity," Mr Fedgewick said. "He did say, however, that he might be a little late."

"Who said?" Stephanie's father asked, and the solicitor looked down at the file open before him.

"A most unusual name, this," he said. "It seems we are waiting on one Mr Skulduggery Pleasant."

"Well who on earth is that?" asked Beryl, irritated. "He sounds like a, he sounds like a... Fergus, what does he sound like?"

"He sounds like a weirdo," Fergus said, glaring at Fedgewick. "He's not a weirdo, is he?"

"I really couldn't say," Fedgewick answered, his paltry excuse for a smile failing miserably under the glares he was getting from Fergus and Beryl. "But I'm sure he'll be along soon."

Fergus frowned, narrowing his beady eyes as much as was possible. "How are you sure?"

Fedgewick faltered, unable to offer a reason, and then the door opened and the man in the tan overcoat entered the room.

"Sorry I'm late," he said, closing the door behind him. "It was unavoidable I'm afraid."

Everyone in the room stared at him, stared at the scarf and the gloves and the sunglasses and the wild fuzzy hair. It was a glorious day outside, certainly not the kind of weather to be wrapped up like this. Stephanie looked closer at the hair. From this distance, it didn't even seem real.

The solicitor cleared his throat. "Um, you are Skulduggery Pleasant?"

"At your service," the man said. Stephanie could listen to that voice all day. Her mother, uncertain as she was, had smiled her greetings, but her father was looking at him with an expression of wariness she had never seen on his face before. After a moment the expression left him and he nodded politely and looked back to Mr Fedgewick. Fergus and Beryl were still staring.

"Do you have something wrong with your face?" Beryl asked.

Fedgewick cleared his throat again. "OK then, let's get down to business, now that we're all here. Excellent. Good. This, of course, being the last will and testament of Gordon Edgley, revised last almost one year ago. Gordon has been a client of mine for the past twenty years, and in that time, I got to know him well, so let me pass on to you, his family and, and friend, my deepest, deepest—"

"Yes yes yes," Fergus interrupted, waving his hand in the air. "Can we just skip this part? We're already running behind schedule. Let's go to the part where we get stuff. Who gets the house? And who gets the villa?"

"Who gets the fortune?" Beryl asked, leaning forward in her seat.

"The royalties," Fergus said. "Who gets the royalties from the books?"

Stephanie glanced at Skulduggery Pleasant from the corner of her eye. He was standing back against the wall, hands in his pockets, looking at the solicitor. Well, he *seemed* to be looking at the solicitor; with those sunglasses he could have been looking anywhere. She returned her gaze to Fedgewick as he picked up a page from his desk and read from it.

"'To my brother Fergus and his beautiful wife Beryl,'" he read, and Stephanie did her best to hide a grin, "'I leave my car, and my boat, and a gift.'"

Fergus and Beryl blinked. "His car?" Fergus said. "His boat? Why would he leave me his boat?"

"You hate the water," Beryl said, anger rising in her voice. "You get seasick."

"I *do* get seasick," Fergus snapped, "and he knew that!"

"And we already have a car," Beryl said.

"And we already have a car!" Fergus repeated.

Beryl was sitting so far up on her chair that she was almost on the desk. "This gift," she said, her voice low and threatening, "is it the fortune?"

Mr Fedgewick coughed nervously, and took a small box from his desk drawer and slid it towards them. They looked at this box. They looked some more. They both reached for it at the same time, and Stephanie watched them slap at each other's hands until Beryl snatched it off the desk and tore the lid open.

"What is it?" Fergus asked in a small voice. "Is it a key to a safety deposit box? Is it, is it an account number? Is it, what is it? Wife, what is it?"

All colour had drained from Beryl's face and her hands were shaking. She blinked hard to keep the tears away, then she turned the box for everyone to see, and everyone saw the brooch, about the size of a drinks coaster, nestled in the plush cushion. Fergus stared at it.

"It doesn't even have any jewels on it," Beryl said, her voice strangled. Fergus opened his mouth wide like a startled fish and turned to Fedgewick.

"What else do we get?" he asked, panicking.

Mr Fedgewick tried another smile. "Your, uh, your brother's love?"

Stephanie heard a high-pitched whine, and it took her a moment to realise it was coming from Beryl. Fedgewick returned his attention to the will, trying to ignore the horrified looks he was getting from Fergus and his wife.

"'To my good friend and guide Skulduggery Pleasant I leave the following advice. Your path is your own, and I have no wish to sway you, but sometimes the greatest enemy we can face is ourselves, and the greatest battle is against the darkness within. There is a storm coming, and sometimes the key to safe harbour is hidden from us, and sometimes it is right before our eyes.'"

Stephanie joined in with everyone else as they stared at Mr Pleasant. She had known there was something different about him, she had known it the first moment she saw him – there was something exotic, something mysterious, something *dangerous*. For his part, his head dipped lower and that was the only reaction he gave. He offered no explanations as to what Gordon's message had meant.

Fergus patted his wife's knee. "See, Beryl? A car, a boat, a brooch, it's not that bad. He could have given us some stupid advice."

WORLD BOOK DAY

HOW DO YOU SHARE STORIES?

What's the **GREATEST BOOK** you've ever read, the most **POWERFUL STORY** ever told?

Which **AUTHOR** speaks to you the loudest, who is the **CHARACTER** that **STUCK IN YOUR HEAD** long after you put the book down?

Which **ILLUSTRATORS** enchant you and make you want to pick up a pen yourself?

How do you get your **BOOKISH** fix? Downloaded to your phone or do you prefer the feel of a book in your hands?

Here at WORLD BOOK DAY, we celebrate books in all their glory and guises, we love to think and talk about books. Did you know we are a charity, here to bring books, your favourite authors and illustrators and much more to readers like you?

We believe **BOOKS AND READING ARE A GIFT**, and this book is our gift to **YOU**.

#WORLDBOOKDAY

From breakfast to bedtime, there's always time to discover and share stories together. You can . . .

1 TAKE A TRIP TO YOUR LOCAL BOOKSHOP

Brimming with brilliant books and helpful booksellers to share awesome reading recommendations, you can also enjoy booky events with your favourite authors and illustrators.

Find your local bookshop:
booksellers.org.uk/bookshopsearch

2 JOIN YOUR LOCAL LIBRARY

That wonderful place where the hugest selection of books you could ever want to read awaits – and you can borrow them for FREE! Plus expert advice and fantastic free family reading events.

Find your local library:
gov.uk/local-library-services/

3 CHECK OUT THE WORLD BOOK DAY WEBSITE

Looking for reading tips, advice and inspiration? There is so much to discover at worldbookday.com, packed with videos, activities, interviews with your favourite authors and illustrators, all the latest book news and much more.

SPONSORED BY

Changing lives through a love of books and shared reading.

World Book Day is a registered charity funded by publishers and booksellers in the UK & Ireland.